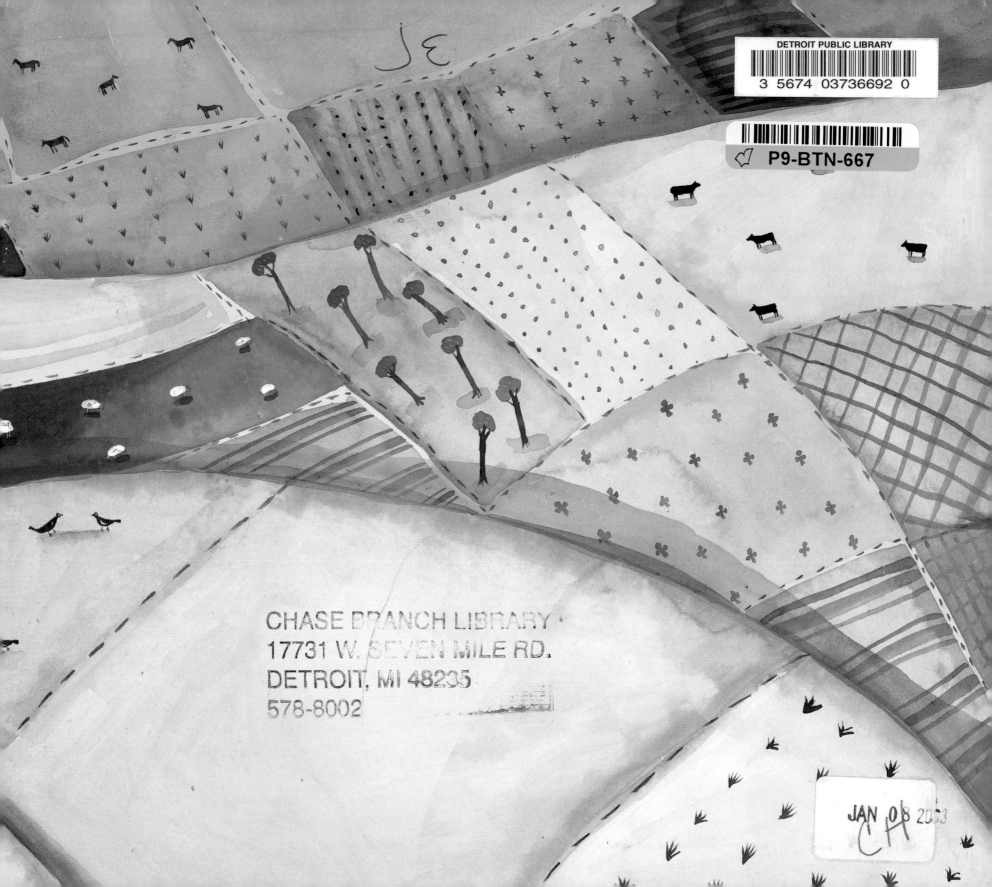

For Polly Meynell
—M. P. O.

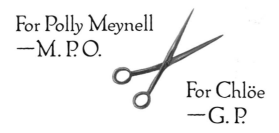

For Chlöe
—G. P.

Author's Note

The Brave Little Seamstress is a reworking of the German tale "The Brave Little Tailor," one of many
fairy tales collected by the Brothers Grimm in the early 1800s. According to Joseph Campbell, the tale was
originally told to the Grimm brothers by female relatives Jeannette and Amalie Hassenpflug. I consulted
several translations of the Grimm's tale but relied primarily on Andrew Lang, who retold a number of fairy
tales in books published from 1889 to 1913. Cary Wilkins, in an introduction to *The Andrew Lang Fairy
Tale Treasury,* says that Lang was not responsible for most of the retellings and translations of the fairy tales
in his books. That work was done "by his wife, his cousins, his wife's nieces, and other literary young women."
This fact—along with the fact that the tale was originally told to the Grimm brothers by two women—
makes turning the little tailor into a little seamstress seem even more apt.

Atheneum Books for Young Readers
An imprint of Simon & Schuster Children's Publishing Division
1230 Avenue of the Americas
New York, NY 10020
Text copyright © 2002 by Mary Pope Osborne
Illustrations copyright © 2002 by Giselle Potter
Book design by Ann Bobco
The text of this book is set in Packard OP.
The illustrations are rendered in pencil, ink, gouache, gesso,
and watercolor.
Printed in Hong Kong
10 9 8 6 5 4 3 2 1

Library of Congress Cataloging-in-Publication Data
Osborne, Mary Pope.
The brave little seamstress / by Mary Pope Osborne ; illustrated by
Giselle Potter.
p. cm.
Summary: A seamstress who kills seven flies with one blow outwits the
king and, with the help of a kind knight, becomes a wise and kind
queen.
ISBN 0-689-84486-7
[1. Fairy tales.] I. Potter, Giselle, ill. II. Brave little tailor. English. III.
Title.

PZ8+
[E]—dc21
2001033018

THE BRAVE LITTLE SEAMSTRESS

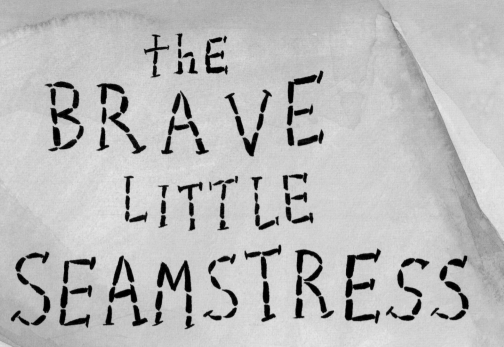

Written by
Mary Pope Osborne

illustrated by
Giselle Potter

An Anne Schwartz Book
Atheneum Books for Young Readers

NEW YORK   LONDON   TORONTO   SYDNEY   SINGAPORE

One summer day a little seamstress sat by her window, eating bread and jam. When the jam attracted a swarm of flies, she tried to wave them away.

Shoo!

Go Away!

But the flies, who didn't speak English, kept coming back. Finally the little seamstress lost her patience. She grabbed a cloth and swung it at the windowsill.

"Take that!" she said.

When she looked down, she saw she had slain no fewer than seven flies.

"Goodness!" the little seamstress said. "I've killed seven flies with one blow. Imagine that." And to mark the event, she took out her favorite coat and stitched on the back:

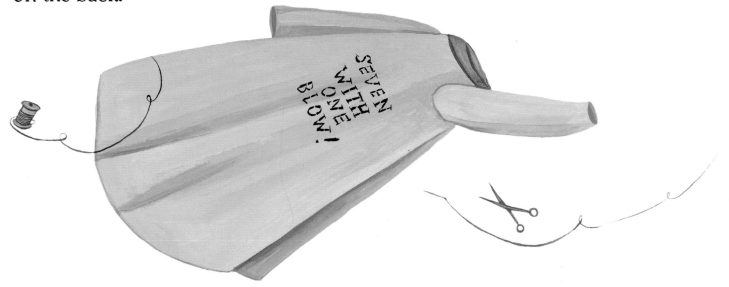

SEVEN WITH ONE BLOW!

As she stitched each word, the little seamstress grew prouder and prouder of her amazing feat. Her heart wagged with joy like the tail of a lamb.

By the time she'd stitched the *w* in *blow,* she had come to believe that her little workshop was far too small to contain such valor. "The whole town should hear of this," she exclaimed. "No! The whole world should hear!"

The little seamstress grabbed a chunk of old cheese for provisions and a gray bird who lived in her yard for company. Then she set out into the world.

Following her nose, the little seamstress walked out of her village and up a mountain. At the top sat a huge, powerful giant.

"Good day, friend," the little seamstress said boldly. Then she walked slowly past, so the giant could read the words stitched on her coat:

SEVEN WITH ONE BLOW!

"Humph," said the giant, for he assumed she was claiming to have slain seven *giants* with one blow. "Hey!" he bellowed.

The little seamstress turned. "Yes?"

The giant picked up a rock and squeezed
it with his huge hand until drops of water
dripped out. Then he smiled proudly at the
little seamstress. "Can you do *that*?" he asked.

"Of course," she replied. She thought fast,
then reached into her pocket and pulled out
the hunk of old cheese.

"Ah, here's a good hard rock," she said.

The little seamstress squeezed the cheese
until its liquid ran through her fingers.
"There," she said.

"Humph," said the giant.

He picked up a stone and hurled it into the air. The stone sailed high over the trees and landed in a distant field.

The giant smiled proudly at the little seamstress. "Can you do *that*?" he asked.

"Of course," she replied. She thought fast, then reached into her pocket and pulled out the gray bird. "Ah, here's a good stone," she said.

The little seamstress tossed the gray bird high into the air, and it flew up, up, over the trees, over the field — and out of sight.

"There," she said.

"Humph," said the giant.

He pointed to a mighty fallen oak that lay across their path. "If you're so strong," he said, "carry that giant tree down the mountain with me."

"That teeny sapling?" said the little seamstress. She thought fast, then pointed to the base of the trunk. "You take the end with those spindly roots, and I'll take the heavy end with the branches."

The giant smiled, certain he was getting the best of the bargain.

Groaning, he hoisted the trunk onto his shoulder—
while, unbeknownst to him, the little seamstress jumped
nimbly onto the branches.

The little seamstress sang a merry song as the giant hauled the entire
tree by himself—roots, trunk, branches, little singing seamstress, and all!

When the giant could go no farther, he dropped the tree—*Boom!*—
and wiped his brow. "I have to stop," he said.

The little seamstress sprang down and grabbed some branches, as if
she'd been carrying half the tree all along. "I could keep going forever,"
she said cheerfully, "but since you're so weary, I'll leave you to rest."

And so the little seamstress went on her way. She followed her nose until she came to a gleaming palace. Feeling quite sleepy, she lay down in the courtyard to take a nap.

She had been asleep only a few minutes when one of the king's horsemen passed by. He read the words stitched on her coat, then rushed to tell the king what he had seen.

The king came at once. "*Seven with one blow? Incredible!*" he cried, for he thought the little seamstress was claiming to have slain seven *knights* with one blow. "This woman warrior has come to take my kingdom! I must find a way to stop her."

The king thought for a moment, then woke the little seamstress.

"Great warrior, welcome to my kingdom," he said. "Perhaps you can help us. Two horrible giants live in the forest nearby."

More giants? thought the little seamstress.

"They are scoundrels, thieves, and murderers," said the king. "If you slay them, I will give you half my kingdom."

Goodness, one is not offered half a kingdom every day, thought the little seamstress. "I'll try," she said.

The brave little
seamstress followed her nose
into the forest. She cast her sharp
eyes left, then right, until she spied the
two horrible giants sleeping under a tree. They
were snoring so heavily, the tree branches waved up
and down above them.

The little seamstress filled her pockets with stones, then
climbed the tree.

Taking careful aim, she dropped a stone onto the head of one of the giants.

Thump!

The giant woke with a start. "Hey!" he yelled at the other giant. "Why did you strike me?"

"I didn't strike you!" said the second giant. "You were dreaming, you fool! Go back to sleep."

Once the giants had fallen asleep again, the little seamstress dropped a stone on the second giant.

Thump!

"Ho!" the giant roared. "Why did you strike me?"

"I didn't strike you!" the first giant said. "Now it's *you* who's dreaming. Go back to sleep."

When the giants had dozed off again, the little seamstress dropped a third stone. It landed on the nose of the first giant.

Thump!

"Hey! You did it again!" the giant shouted. He sprang up and struck the other giant on *his* nose.

Now the giants began to fight in earnest. They tore trees from their roots and swung them at each other. The two fought long and hard until . . .

. . . both dropped dead.

"It's lucky they didn't uproot my tree," the little seamstress said as she climbed down, "or I should have had to spring to another like a squirrel."

The little seamstress returned to the king and led him into the woods. When he saw the fallen trees and the slain giants, he was more amazed than ever.

"You are wondrous!" he exclaimed. "Please, I beg you, help me one more time. Capture the wild unicorn of the wood. It is a great danger to my subjects, for it attacks anyone who crosses its path."

The king thought this would take care of the little seamstress once and for all, for the unicorn was truly vicious.

"Why not?" said the brave little seamstress. "I slew two horrible giants. Why should I be afraid of a wild unicorn? Let's see." She thought for a moment. "Bring me an ax and a rope."

The king's servants brought the ax and rope, and the little seamstress strode off to capture the wild unicorn.

It was not long before she spied the creature. Stepping out from behind an oak, she called out, "Hey! Unicorn!"
The unicorn looked up.
"Over here!" she called and waved her coat.
The wild beast rushed at her with its long, sharp horn.

The little seamstress sprang nimbly back behind the oak. The unicorn kept charging and rammed the point of its horn into the tree trunk.

Bucking frantically, the unicorn tried to free itself. "There, there," soothed the little seamstress, and she used her ax to loose the unicorn's horn.

The grateful creature allowed her to tie the rope around its neck. Then the little seamstress led the unicorn back to the king.

"Amazing!" the king exclaimed. "Could you possibly do just one more thing for my kingdom?"

The little seamstress sighed. She'd begun to fear the king was taking advantage of her helpful nature. "All right, one more feat," she said. "But that will have to be all for today."

"Excellent," said the king. "Could you capture the wild boar who lives near the woodland chapel? He has slain many hunters and several monks."

"Of course I can," said the little seamstress. "I just slew two horrible giants. I tamed a wild unicorn. Why should I be afraid of a wild boar?"

And so she went forth once more into the forest.

It was not long before she spied the wild boar near an abandoned chapel in a clearing. She stepped in front of the open door.

"Hey! Boar!" she shouted.

The boar looked up.

"Over here!" she called and waved her arms.

The boar charged at her with its sharp teeth and gleaming tusks.

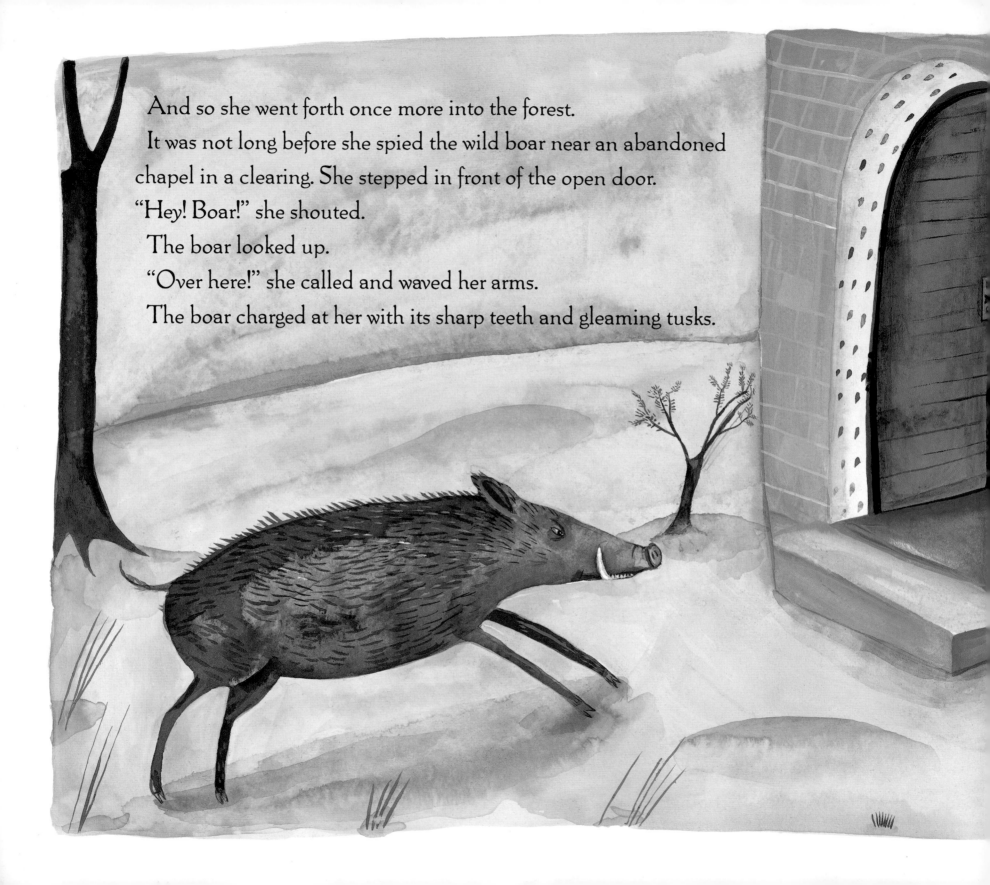

The little seamstress dashed into the chapel and leaped out the back window. When the boar ran inside, the seamstress skipped around to the door and locked it, trapping the raging beast.

Then she returned to the king.

"The giants are slain, the unicorn is tamed, and the wild boar is locked in your chapel," she said. "Now, may I have half your kingdom, please?"

The king saw that he had no choice. "We shall have the ceremony tomorrow," he said, with much regret and little joy.

"Thank you," she said. "And now can someone show me to my chambers? I'm a bit tired."

That night a serving maid heard the little seamstress talking in her sleep. "Yes,
I can mend your trousers by Tuesday next," she mumbled. "It will cost you twenty pence."
The maid was puzzled, so she went to the king and told him what she had heard.

"Good heavens!" said the king. "She's not a woman warrior at all! She's a little seamstress!" The king called a hundred of his strongest knights together and told them to meet him outside the little seamstress's door at midnight. At his signal they would burst into her room, capture her, and carry her to a ship that would take her far away across the sea.

But one of the king's knights so admired the little seamstress's spirit that he slipped down to her chambers, woke her up, and revealed the king's wicked plan. "Goodness!" said the little seamstress. "And after all I've done for him!"

The little seamstress thanked the kind knight and sent him on his way. Then she crawled back into bed. At midnight when she heard the king and his men gather outside her door, she pretended to talk in her sleep.

"Yes, yes, I can mend your trousers, don't worry," she said loudly. "After all, I killed seven with one blow. I crushed a rock with my bare hand. I threw a stone to kingdom come. I slew two horrible giants. I tamed the wild unicorn. I captured the wild boar. WHY SHOULD I BE AFRAID OF A HUNDRED LITTLE MEN HIDING OUTSIDE MY DOOR?"

"Wha-a-t?" cried the king.

"A-HA!" shouted the little seamstress. She leaped out of bed and threw open the door.

Overcome with terror, the king and ninety-nine of his knights ran out of the castle. They jumped on their horses and rode away as fast as they could, never to return.

The hundredth knight stayed behind. He, of course, was the one who had warned the little seamstress of the king's wicked plan.

Not surprisingly, she'd grown quite fond of him. "Will you marry me?" she asked. "Indeed I will," he replied.